To Megs, Krissy, Erin and Jordie with wonderful memories
of your singing and dancing at le Tupé
— love always, Mama

For Tuppence and Aeron — D. H.

Barefoot Books
294 Banbury Road
Oxford, OX2 7ED

Barefoot Books
2067 Massachusetts Ave
Cambridge, MA 02140

Text copyright © 2000 by Barefoot Books. Illustrations copyright © 2000 by Debbie Harter. Music on the accompanying
CD written and performed by Fred Penner. Recording and production by DeCapo Studios, USA in 2002. Animation by
Zachary Bennett, KZ Films, New York. The moral rights of Barefoot Books and Debbie Harter
have been asserted. First published in Great Britain by Barefoot Books, Ltd and in the United
States of America by Barefoot Books, Inc in 2000. All rights reserved. Printed in China on 100%
acid-free paper. This book was typeset in Hip Hop and One Stroke Script Infant
The illustrations were prepared in paint, pen and ink, and crayon

ISBN 978-1-84686-716-3

British Cataloguing-in-Publication Data: a catalogue record for this book is available from the British Library

Library of Congress Cataloging-in-Publication Data is available under LCCN 2005013843

135798642

The Animal Boogie

Illustrated by **Debbie Harter**
Sung by **Fred Penner**

Barefoot Books
Step inside a story

Down in the jungle, come if you dare!
What can you see shaking here and there?
With a shaky shake here and a shaky shake there,
What's that creature shaking here and there?

IT'S A BEAR!

She goes shake, shake, boogie, woogie, oogie!

Shake, shake, boogie, woogie, oogie!

Shake, shake, boogie, woogie, oogie!

That's the way she's shaking here and there.

Down in the jungle where nobody sees,
What can you see swinging through the trees?
With a swingy swing here and a swingy swing there,
What's that creature swinging through the trees?

IT'S A MONKEY!

He goes swing, swing, boogie, woogie, oogie!

Swing, swing, boogie, woogie, oogie!

Swing, swing, boogie, woogie, oogie!

That's the way he's swinging through the trees.

Down in the jungle in the midday heat,
What can you see stomping its feet?
With a stompy stomp here and a stompy stomp there,
What's that creature stomping its feet?

IT'S AN ELEPHANT!
She goes stomp, stomp, boogie, woogie, oogie!
Stomp, stomp, boogie, woogie, oogie!
Stomp, stomp, boogie, woogie, oogie!
That's the way she's stomping her feet.

Down in the jungle where the trees grow high,
What can you see flying in the sky?
With a flappy flap here and a flappy flap there,
What's that creature flying in the sky?

IT'S A BIRD!
He goes flap, flap, boogie, woogie, oogie!
Flap, flap, boogie, woogie, oogie!
Flap, flap, boogie, woogie, oogie!
That's the way he's flying in the sky.

Down in the jungle where the leaves lie deep,
What can you see learning how to leap?
With a leapy leap here and a leapy leap there,
What's that creature learning how to leap?

IT'S A LEOPARD!

She goes leap, leap, boogie, woogie, oogie!

Leap, leap, boogie, woogie, oogie!

Leap, leap, boogie, woogie, oogie!

That's the way she's learning how to leap.

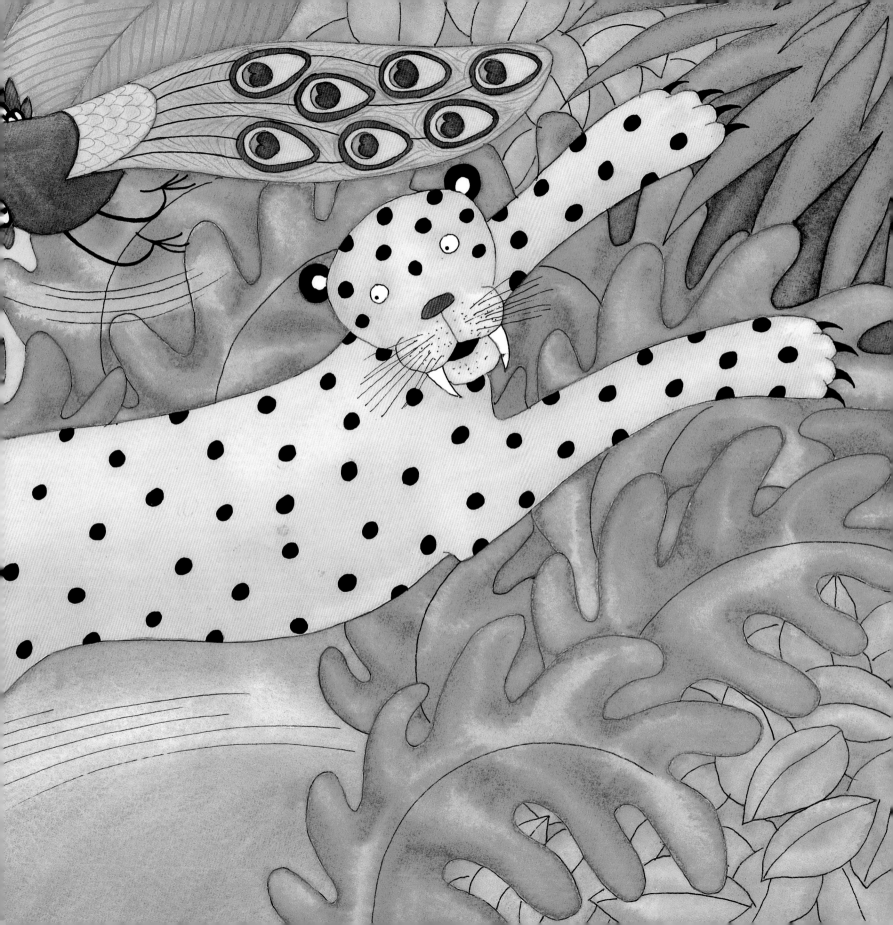

Down in the jungle where there's danger all around,
What can you see slithering on the ground?
With a slither slither here and a slither slither there,
What's that creature slithering on the ground?

IT'S A SNAKE!
He goes slither, slither, boogie, woogie, oogie!
Slither, slither, boogie, woogie, oogie!
Slither, slither, boogie, woogie, oogie!
That's the way he's slithering on the ground!

Down in the jungle where the stars are shining bright,
Who can you see swaying left and right?
With a sway sway here and a sway sway there,
Who is swaying left and swaying right?

WE ARE!
We go sway, sway, boogie, woogie, oogie!
Sway, sway, boogie, woogie, oogie!
Sway, sway, boogie, woogie, oogie!
That's the way we boogie through the night!

let's stomp!
(INDIAN ELEPHANT)

let's slither! (COBRA)

let's boogie!

let's sway!
(PARROTS)

(HORNBILL)

The Animal Boogie

Down in the jun - gle, come if you dare!

What can you see shak - ing here and there? With a

shak - y shake here and a shak - y shake there,

spoken

what's that crea - ture shak - ing here and there? It's a bear! She goes

shake, shake, boog - ie, woog - ie, oo - gie!

Shake, shake, boog - ie, woog - ie, oo - gie!

Shake, shake, boog - ie, woog - ie, oo - gie!

That's the way she's shak - ing here and there.

Barefoot Books
step inside a story